D0970072

Dear Parent:

Your child's love of reading s

Every child learns to read in a different way and at his or her own speed. Some go back and forth between reading levels and read favorite books again and again. Others read through each level in order. You can help your young reader improve and become more confident by encouraging his or her own interests and abilities. From books your child reads with you to the first books he or she reads alone, there are I Can Read Books for every stage of reading:

SHARED READING
Basic language, word repetition, and whimsical illustrations, ideal for sharing with your emergent reader

BEGINNING READING
Short sentences, familiar words, and simple concepts for children eager to read on their own

READING WITH HELP
Engaging stories, longer sentences, and language play for developing readers

READING ALONE
Complex plots, challenging vocabulary, and high-interest topics for the independent reader

I Can Read Books have introduced children to the joy of reading since 1957. Featuring award-winning authors and illustrators and a fabulous cast of beloved characters, I Can Read Books set the standard for beginning readers.

A lifetime of discovery begins with the magical words "I Can Read!"

Visit www.icanread.com for information
on enriching your child's reading experience.

I Can Read® and I Can Read Book® are trademarks of HarperCollins Publishers.

Love, Diana: Boris the School Bully
Copyright © 2022 by PocketWatch, Inc.
All Rights Reserved. Love, Diana and all related titles, logos and characters, and the
pocket.watch logo are trademarks of PocketWatch, Inc. All other rights are the property
of their respective owners. Printed in the United States of America.

Library of Congress Control Number: 2022931763
ISBN 978-0-06-320442-3

22 23 24 25 26 LSCC   10 9 8 7 6 5 4 3 2 1   ❖   First Edition

I Can Read!

1 BEGINNING READING

pocket.watch

Love, Diana™

Boris the School Bully

HARPER

An Imprint of HarperCollinsPublishers

It's a beautiful day at school
for Diana and Roma.
But look!

4

Boris and his boring bullies

have come to ruin recess.

It's up to Diana and Roma
to save the day.
Diana becomes
the Princess of Play.
Roma becomes
the Prince of Pretend!

Mean old Boris won't let
Koko enjoy her book.
Boris gets a kick out of
ripping up the pages.

Koko is just a small kittycorn.

She starts to cry.

Roma wants to fight Boris.

But Diana knows fighting

with a bully never solves anything.

Two wrongs don't make a right.

But just then, Boris throws the book.

It lands on Roma's head.

Roma is annoyed

but he knows Diana is right.

Boris isn't the only one

being a bully.

Blubber is causing trouble too!

He likes to pick on
anyone smaller than him.
Even little gophers!

Roma makes sure no one gets hurt.

The gophers want to fight back too.

But Roma teaches them

what Diana taught him:

Never stoop to a bully's level.

BANG!

Diana and Roma race over

to the lockers.

It sounds like someone is stuck inside!

Diana and Roma can't open the locker.

Boris and the bullies laugh.

Their plan to take over

the playground is working!

Look!

Dawn, the Duchess of Daring,

arrives just in time!

Dawn tosses a hair pin to Diana.

Now they can open the lockers.

With Dawn's help,
Diana and Roma
rescue their friends.

Boris and his minions
laugh about all the
trouble they have caused.
But not for long!

Honey is angry with the bullies

for trapping her in the locker.

She scares them by kicking her legs.

But Diana is upset.

She knows that being mean

to a bully makes you a bully too.

Diana thinks the bullies are mean because they never feel included. She plays a song on her boom box and invites Boris and the others to join the fun!

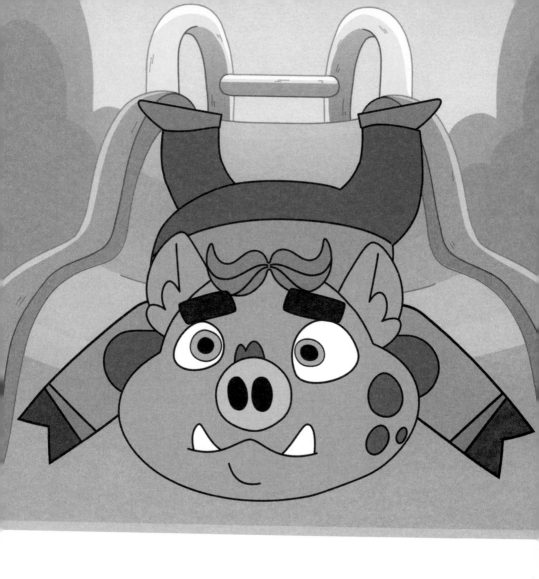

Could it be?

Boris and his minions actually

enjoy playing with everyone else!

They are still learning

how to share and get along,

but maybe they don't

have to be bullies after all.

For a moment,

Diana really thinks she has changed

Boris's mind about being a bully.

But then the bullies remember
that they hate getting along.
Boris and his minions run away.

Well, at least everyone *else* can enjoy the rest of recess. The Princess of Play has saved the day!